Disney
The Never Girls

the
woods
beyond

Written by
Kiki Thorpe

Illustrated by
Jana Christy

A STEPPING STONE BOOK
RANDOM HOUSE 🏠 NEW YORK

For the readers at Hancock Elementary,
who asked for a story with boys
—K.T.

For Jim Christy, my awesome dad
—J.C.

Published in the United States by Random House Children's Books,
a division of Random House, LLC., 1745 Broadway, New York, NY 10019,
and in Canada by Random House of Canada Limited, Toronto, Penguin Random
House Companies, in conjunction with Disney Enterprises, Inc. Random House
and the colophon are registered trademarks and A Stepping Stone Book and the
colophon are trademarks of Random House LLC.

Library of Congress Cataloging-in-Publication Data
Thorpe, Kiki.
The woods beyond / written by Kiki Thorpe ; illustrated by Jana Christy.
pages cm. — (The Never girls ; 6)
"A Stepping Stone book."
Summary: Lainey's bad day turns worse when Prilla the fairy calls her clumsy, but
while walking in the woods of Never Land, Lainey discovers the hideout of the
Lost Boys and makes some new friends.
ISBN 978-0-7364-3096-8 (trade) — ISBN 978-0-7364-8148-9 (lib. bdg.) —
ISBN 978-0-7364-3221-4 (ebook)
[1. Fairies—Fiction. 2. Magic—Fiction. 3. Friendship—Fiction.] I. Christy, Jana,
illustrator. II. Title.
PZ7.T3974Woo 2014
[Fic]—dc23
2013040893

randomhouse.com/kids/disney
Printed in the United States of America
10 9 8 7 6 5

Never Land

Far away from the world we know, on the distant seas of dreams, lies an island called Never Land. It is a place full of magic, where mermaids sing, fairies play, and children never grow up. Adventures happen every day, and anything is possible.

There are two ways to reach Never Land. One is to find the island yourself. The other is for it to find you. Finding Never Land on your own takes a lot of luck and a pinch of fairy dust. Even then, you will only find the island if it wants to be found.

Every once in a while, Never Land drifts close to our world . . . so close a fairy's laugh slips through. And every once in an even longer while, Never Land opens its doors to a special few. Believing in magic and fairies from the bottom of your heart can make the extraordinary happen. If you suddenly hear tiny bells or feel a sea breeze where there is no sea, pay careful attention. Never Land may be close by. You could find yourself there in the blink of an eye.

One day, four special girls came to Never Land in just this way. This is their story.

Never Land

Pirate Cove

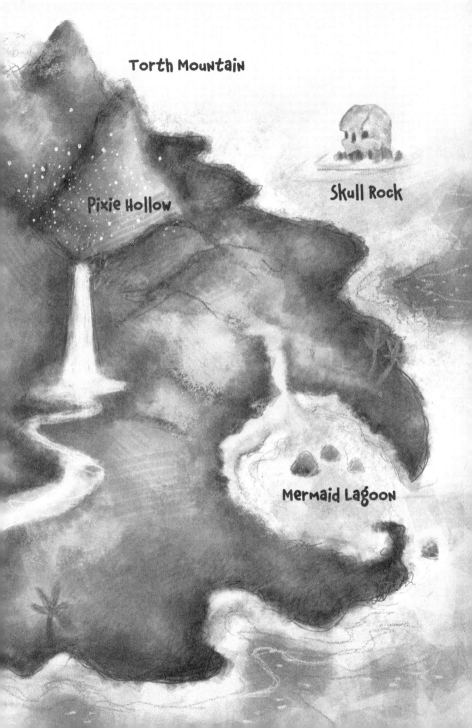

Chapter 1

Ever since four friends—Lainey Winters, Kate McCrady, Mia Vasquez, and Mia's little sister, Gabby—discovered a secret passage to Never Land, each day held the possibility of a new adventure. Mornings, they woke up feeling like the luckiest girls in the world. Most mornings, that is.

"Lainey!"

Lainey Winters opened her eyes. Her mother was calling her. She reached out, feeling around for her glasses. Her hand touched the wooden nightstand where she always left them.

But her glasses weren't there.

"Lainey!" her mother yelled again. "Come down here!"

Lainey got out of bed. Without her glasses, everything looked blurry. Where could she have left them?

As she fumbled across the room, she stubbed her toe, hard. "Ow!" Lainey cried. Blinking back tears, she hopped on one foot to her dresser and felt around on top. Her glasses weren't there, either.

The bedroom door opened. "Didn't you hear me?" her mother asked. "I've been calling you for the last five minutes." She frowned. "Where are your glasses?"

"I don't know." Lainey looked around helplessly. "Somewhere . . ."

"Not another lost pair," her mother said with a sigh. "You'll have to wear the spare ones."

It was Lainey's turn to frown. She *hated* her spare glasses. Her regular big, square glasses were bad enough. But the spare ones were broken and had been fixed with tape. In Lainey's opinion, they just looked *dumb.*

"When you're ready, come downstairs. There's something I want you to see." Her mother left.

Lainey found the old glasses in her desk drawer. *Why couldn't these be lost?* she wondered. Then she got dressed and went downstairs. Her mother was standing in the kitchen with her arms folded across her chest.

"Look outside," she said to Lainey.

Lainey looked out the window. "Oh no!" she exclaimed.

In front of their house, the garbage and recycling cans lay on their sides. The trash bags inside had been ripped open, and garbage was scattered around their yard. More trash was strewn along the sidewalk. "What happened?" Lainey asked.

"Some animals must have gotten into

the trash," her mother replied. "Raccoons, probably. Did you leave those dishes out last night, Lainey?"

She was talking about Lainey's dog bowls. Every morning in the summertime, Lainey filled two big bowls with dog food and water and left them on the sidewalk in front of their house for any hungry or thirsty dogs that passed. Lainey didn't have a dog, but she tried to get to know all the pets in her neighborhood. She liked to help out her furry friends whenever she could.

Lainey's parents didn't share her love of animals. Because they didn't want a pet of their own, they didn't mind the bowls. But the rule was that she had to bring them in at night.

And she *had* brought them in, hadn't she?

Lainey leaned closer to the window. By standing on her tiptoes, she could see down the front stoop. Two metal bowls were sitting by the bottom step—right where she'd left them.

"I'm sorry, Mom," Lainey said. "I guess I forgot."

Her mother sighed. "Sweetie, I think it's wonderful that you want to help the neighborhood dogs. But I told you that dog food could attract other animals, ones we *don't* want around. And now we have a problem. We can't just leave all that trash out there."

"I'll pick it up," Lainey said. "It's my fault. Just please let me keep the bowls."

Her mother considered this, then

nodded. "All right. But you'll need to clean up right after breakfast. You have swimming lessons this morning."

"Swim lessons!" Lainey groaned. That was even worse than having to pick up the trash. Every summer, her mother signed her up for swim classes at the community pool, even though Lainey begged her not to. "But I'm supposed to go over to Mia's this morning," she said.

"You can go to Mia's in the afternoon," said her mom. "You're there all the time as it is. What do you girls do all day? You always come back with leaves in your hair and sand in your shoes, as if you've been trekking to Timbuktu."

Not Timbuktu. Never Land, thought Lainey. But she shrugged and said, "We're just . . . you know, playing."

Her mother smiled and ruffled Lainey's hair. "All right. Hurry and eat breakfast. We have to leave for the pool by nine."

After breakfast, Lainey went outside armed with two big garbage bags and a pair of rubber dishwashing gloves. She looked around at the mess.

Lainey's front lawn wasn't large—just a gated courtyard in front of her row house. But the area was covered with coffee grounds, potato peels, plastic wrap, eggshells, crumpled paper towels, used tissues, and moldy leftovers. More trash was scattered all the way down the sidewalk.

Lainey wrinkled her nose. She wished she could find the animals that did this. She'd give them a good talking-to!

With a sigh, Lainey snapped open a garbage bag and got to work. A slimy head of lettuce brushed against her arm. A milk carton dribbled sour milk onto her jeans.

"Yuck! Double yuck!" Lainey held her breath and kept going. As she worked, she imagined she was already in Pixie Hollow. How much better things were there! She could go for a ride on the back of a deer. Or she could help the herding-talent fairies round up the butterflies. Or watch her animal-talent friend Fawn tend to a new-born fox.

Lainey dragged the full bags back to the trash cans just as her mom came out of the house. "Time to go!" she told Lainey.

A horrible hour of swimming followed. As usual, the pool was too crowded and the water was too cold. The instructor kept telling Lainey to put her face in the water. Lainey was an excellent dog paddler. But every time she dunked her head, she got scared and stopped swimming. It didn't help that all the other kids in the class slipped underwater as easily as fishes. By the time class was over, Lainey was embarrassed, shivering, and miserable.

It was almost eleven o'clock when she got home. Although Mia and Gabby's house was only at the end of the block, Lainey didn't want to lose a second. She ran full-speed and arrived out of breath.

The other girls were in the living room. Pillows were spread out on the floor, and they each stood on one. Lainey saw that they were playing Snapping Turtles, a game Gabby had made up. The object was to jump from one pillow to another to avoid the snapping turtles in the "water"— the floor. Gabby loved the game, but the older girls played only when they were desperately bored.

"Finally!" Kate exclaimed when she saw Lainey.

"We've been waiting for *ages*!" Mia added.

"Mia! You stepped off your pillow!" Gabby cried. "The snapping turtles got you!"

"Who cares?" Mia said, giving her pillow a little kick. "The game is over." She put her hands on her hips. "Where have you been?" she asked Lainey.

"I . . . well, I . . . ," Lainey stammered.

"Why is your hair wet?" asked Gabby.

"Did you just get out of the shower or something?" asked Kate.

"Don't tell me you slept in!" Mia exclaimed.

Lainey's heart sank. Even her best friends were annoyed with her. "I didn't sleep in!" she wailed. "I had swimming lessons. And before that I had to pick up all the garbage—"

"Never mind," said Kate impatiently. "At least you're here now. We can go to *Never Land*." She said the last two words in a whisper.

"Come on," said Gabby. "Let's hurry!"

Lainey's mood lifted as they raced up the stairs to Gabby's room, where the magical passage lay behind a closet door. Visiting Never Land was like opening a present. There was always an adventure waiting. The surprise was finding out what it would be.

   It will all be okay now, Lainey told herself as she stepped into the closet. *Everything will be better once we get to Pixie Hollow.*

chapter 2

That morning in Pixie Hollow, on a high branch of the Home Tree, the fairy Prilla awoke with a start. She looked around her room.

Something had woken her. What could it have been?

Then she heard it. *Crunch. Crunch. Crunch.* The sound seemed to be coming from inside her closet.

Prilla got out of bed and tiptoed across the room. Her closet was a little nook in the wall covered by a maple leaf. She stopped in front of it and listened.

No doubt about it. There was something inside. Taking a deep breath, she pulled back the leaf.

"Ahh!" she screamed. A fat green caterpillar sat in the middle of the closet, chomping on her favorite rose-petal dress.

"Shoo!" Prilla yelled. "Scram!" The caterpillar didn't budge. She threw a slipper at it. The caterpillar ignored her. It finished nibbling a hole through her dress, then started on a tulip skirt.

"Stop, you!" Prilla screamed, throwing the other slipper.

"Prilla? Are you all right?" Beck called through her front door.

Prilla ran to let her in. Beck was an animal-talent fairy. Maybe she could help.

"Hullo!" Beck said when she saw the caterpillar. "How did he get in here?"

"I must have left the window open— Hey, stop that!" Prilla yelled at the caterpillar, who was now nibbling a daisy sundress.

"Shh! Not so loud," said Beck. "Caterpillars don't like loud noise."

"But he's eating my clothes!"

"Well, he's hungry," Beck said. "Can't you see he's about to make a cocoon? That's why he's so fat. He needs a lot of food right now. Don't you, big fella?" She scratched the caterpillar on the back.

Prilla frowned. She'd thought Beck might be a *bit* more helpful. "I'll have to ask the sewing fairies to remake everything," she said.

"They won't be able to make anything

today," Beck replied. "It's Great Games Day."

"Oh no!" cried Prilla. How could she have forgotten? Great Games Day was a rare and exciting event. Fairies of every talent competed to show off their skills. There was a leapfrog race for the animal-talent fairies and an obstacle course for the fast fliers. On the rapids of Havendish Stream, the water fairies held a leaf-boat rodeo. Sewing fairies made fanciful hats, and baking fairies whipped up elaborate cakes. There were poppy seeds to snack on and sunberry punch to drink, and a huge roasted sweet potato for everyone to share. All the fairies dressed up in their best leaf or flower.

And now Prilla's favorite clothes had caterpillar holes in them!

Once Beck had coaxed the tubby bug out the door, Prilla turned back to her closet. The caterpillar had nibbled everything except for one wilted poppy dress in the back.

Prilla had never liked the poppy dress. The sleeves were too tight and the petals drooped. But it would have to do.

It was late by the time Prilla made it to the tearoom for breakfast. Her favorite honey buns were gone, and so was almost everything else. Normally, the baking fairies would have made more. But Prilla knew they were hard at work on their Games Day cakes.

Just as she reached for the last scone, a hand shot out and grabbed it. Prilla turned and saw the fast-flying fairy Vidia.

"Vidia!" Prilla said. "I was about to take that!"

"A bit slow, though, weren't you?" said Vidia. "The quickest hawk gets the mouse, as the saying goes."

"But you have plenty to eat." Prilla pointed to Vidia's plate, which was piled high with breakfast treats.

"Yes, but I need a big breakfast," Vidia replied. "*I'm* competing today. I don't think you can say the same."

Prilla felt her face turn red. Vidia was right. She wasn't part of Great Games Day. Fairies of the same talent always competed against each other, but there were no other fairies with a talent like Prilla's.

Prilla could travel to the mainland— the world of humans—in the blink of an eye and visit children everywhere. She was proud of her talent, for it kept children's belief in fairies alive—and that kept the fairies' magic alive. But sometimes, on days like today, Prilla wished her talent weren't so unusual.

"Well, I'm off to win a race," said Vidia. "Have fun watching." With a swish of her pointed wings, she flew away.

Smarting from Vidia's remark, Prilla sat down at the table. There was hot tea, at least, thank goodness. She poured herself a cup and sighed. *What an awful morning. But I guess that means the day can only get better,* she told herself, taking a sip.

"Ow!" Prilla winced. She'd burned her tongue.

*

After her tea, Prilla flew down to Havendish Stream. All along the banks, fairies were getting ready for the games. The animal-talent fairies were saddling up their frogs. Downstream, water fairies were hoisting their leaf-sails. On the far bank, garden fairies were warming up for the carrot toss.

Watching the excitement only made Prilla feel more left out.

I'll go on a blink, she decided. When she was feeling down, nothing lifted her spirits like visiting children.

Prilla found a quiet spot in the crook between two tree roots, not far from the frogs. She sat down, settling her wilted poppy dress around her. Then she blinked.

In an instant, Pixie Hollow was gone. Prilla was hovering outside a large, white house. Four children in swimsuits were running around in the grass, squirting each other with a garden hose.

Prilla flew over to them. "Clap if you believe in fairies!" she cried.

But the kids didn't clap. They didn't even notice her. They were too busy laughing and running. A girl grabbed the hose and turned it on her friends. They screamed as water rained down on them.

Prilla tried again. She circled above them, saying, "Clap if you be—"

Before she could finish, a blast of water knocked her out of the air.

With a gasp, Prilla was back in Pixie Hollow. By some miracle, her wings were still dry. Otherwise, she was soaked from head to toe, and shivering. But it wasn't from the cold—it was from embarrassment. Those kids hadn't even looked at her!

It was just bad luck, she thought. *The next blink will be better.*

Prilla dried herself off on a dandelion. Then she blinked again. This time she found herself in a wide green field of grass. A group of kids was running toward her.

Prilla smiled and started to greet them. But they ran by without so much as a glance. Then she heard a *thump.* A soccer ball was sailing through the air. It was headed right for her!

In a blink, Prilla was back at the tree root. Her heart was racing. She was furious with herself. Twice she'd blinked—and twice she'd failed.

I should give up, she thought. But that only made her feel worse. Her talent was visiting children—and that was what she was going to do!

Prilla didn't always have control over who she visited on a blink. Usually, that was how she liked it—she met so many more children that way. But now she tried to focus. "Let it be just one kid this time," she said. "Just one boy or girl."

Prilla blinked. She was in a brown room. It had brown curtains, brown carpet, and a brown couch. A young boy lay on the floor with his chin in his hands. He was watching TV.

Prilla flew over to him. "Clap if you believe in fairies!" she exclaimed.

Lost in his show, the boy didn't look up.

Prilla darted in front of his nose. The boy waved a hand, as if swatting a bug. His eyes never moved from the screen.

Tears of anger and frustration sprang to Prilla's eyes. She began to fly circles in front of the boy. "Hey!" she shouted. "Hey! Do you see me?" Prilla waved her hands. She blew a raspberry. She turned a cartwheel in the air.

Finally, she caught the boy's attention. His eyes widened and his mouth formed an O.

Prilla grinned. *At last!* "Clap if you believe—"

"Watch out!" a voice screamed.

Prilla jerked back in surprise. But it wasn't the boy who had cried out. The call had come from far away, in Never Land. Something was wrong.

Prilla snapped back to Pixie Hollow. The scene before her was chaos.

A giant was blundering along the bank of Havendish Stream. Prilla's mind was still on her blink, so it took her a moment to recognize Lainey. The frogs were in a frenzy, hopping up and down the banks as their fairy riders chased after them. Lainey was trying to catch the frogs, too. But she only seemed to be making things worse.

"Don't worry, I've got him!" Lainey yelled as she closed in on a frightened frog.

"Lainey, no!" a fairy cried. But Lainey was trying so hard to catch the frog, she didn't seem to hear.

When Prilla was coming out of a blink, she always felt a bit fuzzy, and she was slow to react. It wasn't until Lainey was almost on top of her that Prilla realized she was about to get stepped on!

"Stop, Lainey! STOP! *STOP!*" Prilla screamed.

Lainey drew up short. Her foot hovered just inches above Prilla.

A look of horror crossed Lainey's face. "Oh my gosh!" she said. "I didn't see you. I'm sorry, Prilla! I'm so sorry!"

Almost getting squished was the last straw. Prilla's bad mood suddenly bubbled over, and she burst out, "Lainey, you must be the *clumsiest* Clumsy who ever lived!"

Lainey looked stunned. She turned and stumbled away.

Prilla regretted her words at once. "Lainey—" she called after her.

But it was too late. Lainey was gone.

Chapter 3

Lainey sat alone beneath the branches of the weeping willow. She hadn't cried once that whole terrible morning. But now the tears flowed down her cheeks.

Everything was wrong. Lainey's bad day hadn't gotten better in Never Land. It had gotten worse—much, *much* worse. To think she'd almost stepped on Prilla . . .

Lainey squeezed her eyes shut. Try as she might, she couldn't erase Prilla's words: "You must be the *clumsiest* Clumsy who ever lived!"

Outside the willow, she heard fairy laughter. Normally, Lainey loved the bell-like sound, but today it made her cringe. Were they laughing at her? By now everyone in Pixie Hollow would have heard what happened. *They're probably all talking about what a big, dumb Clumsy I am,* Lainey thought.

Lainey got to her feet. She couldn't stay here. She wasn't sure she'd ever be able to face her fairy friends again. But where could she go?

The willow room was where the girls had slept their first night in Pixie Hollow. Now they mainly used it as a place to keep things. There were daisy chains Mia had made with the weaving-talent fairies and seashells Gabby had collected on the shores of Never Land.

Lainey spotted her deer harness hanging from a peg on the tree's trunk. The animal-talent fairy Fawn had given Lainey the harness after a particularly rough deer ride.

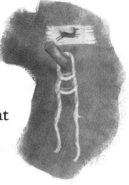

I'll find a deer, Lainey decided. *I'll ride and ride till I'm as far away as I can get.* Just the thought made her feel a little better.

Lainey had never been deer riding without Fawn. In fact, she'd never been in the forest on her own. But that didn't stop her. Grabbing the harness, she ducked outside and looked around.

Just beyond the willow was a deer trail that led into the woods. Lainey followed it. The trail was no more than a matted-down path through the forest undergrowth. It disappeared in some places, only to pick up again in another spot. Sometimes Lainey wasn't sure she was following the same trail, or even following a trail at all. But the woods were quiet and peaceful, and it felt good to walk.

A bird whistled, and Lainey whistled back. She crossed a little stream, where silvery fish flashed in the shallows. Lainey stuck her hand into the cool water and watched them scatter. A tiny frog, no bigger than a walnut, hopped along the bank. Lainey picked it up and cupped it in her hands, feeling its little heart beating.

As she set the frog back in the water,

Lainey had the feeling she was being watched. Slowly, she lifted her head. A black-eyed doe was staring at her from behind the trees.

Her deer! Lainey jumped to her feet. The movement startled the deer and it darted away.

"Wait! Please wait!" Lainey cried, chasing after it.

The doe bounded down a slope. Lainey followed. But she lost her footing on the steep hill. The harness fell from her hand. She tumbled the rest of the way down and landed in a pricker bush.

"Oww!" Lainey tried to get up. Each little movement only made the thorns dig in more. She was stuck!

As she wondered what to do, she heard a voice say, "You're a pudding head!"

Lainey looked around, startled. Through the leaves of the bramble she spied two red, pointed ears. They looked like the ears of a fox.

"If a bear and a lion got in a fight, the lion would definitely win," the voice went on.

"No way!" said a second voice. "I'm telling you, the *bear* would win."

Lainey shifted and caught a glimpse of a rabbit's fluffy white tail.

"Would not!"

"Would so!"

"Would not!"

An electric thrill went through her. All her life Lainey had wanted to talk with animals. She longed to know their feelings and thoughts. And here at last were two she could understand perfectly!

But she was still stuck. Frantically, she tried to get out of the pricker bush. The thorns scratched her skin and tore at her clothes. She could hear the rabbit and fox moving away, still arguing.

Gritting her teeth, Lainey tore herself free. But by the time she reached the place where the animals had been, they were gone.

Lainey stomped her foot in frustration. Where could they have gone so quickly? She began to scour the area for a hole or a burrow, any place an animal might hide.

Not far away was a holly tree studded with bright red berries. There was a hollow in its trunk. *Just the sort of cozy home an animal might like,* Lainey thought.

She went over to the tree and peered inside. The hollow was bigger than she expected. She couldn't see the bottom.

"Hello?" Lainey called. "Anyone there?"

Were her eyes playing tricks on her? Or did she see a faint light somewhere deep down? With her hands stretched out in front of her, Lainey leaned in farther. . . .

She slid down through the tree!

"Oof!" she grunted as she tumbled into a dim chamber.

When her eyes adjusted, she saw that she was in a little room. The ceiling was a network of tree roots. Some of the roots had grown into the room and had been cleverly crafted into furniture. The four posts of the wide bed were made from roots as thick around as Lainey's leg. A wash-basin made from a giant tortoise shell was wedged between two roots. Fresh spring-water trickled into it from a hole.

A hearth had been dug from the dirt wall. A few coals still glowed inside it—this must have been the light Lainey had seen. In the center of the room was a table made from an old stump. Mushrooms big

enough to sit on surrounded it. Lainey tried a mushroom stool and found it quite comfortable. Bowls made from gourds sat on the table. Lainey peeked into one, but it held only water.

Everything was made for someone just about Lainey's size. It was a wonderfully cozy home, though it didn't seem like the house of a fox or a rabbit. She wondered whose it was.

A terrible thought struck her. What if the house belonged to a troll or some other wicked creature?

She heard voices overhead. They seemed to be just outside the entrance.

Lainey didn't want to be caught standing there. She looked for an escape, but the hollow was the only exit. Beneath the bed, there was a narrow gap between the mattress and the floor. Getting down on her belly, Lainey squeezed into it.

And not a moment too soon. A second later, a furry creature rolled into the room.

It got to its feet and stood with its back to Lainey. Was it a troll? Lainey couldn't be sure. It had fur like a bear. But it stood upright.

Lainey heard a scuffling noise as several more creatures came tumbling down through the tree. As one stood, she caught a glimpse of its face.

Lainey gasped. It wasn't a fox or a bear *or* a troll. It was a boy!

Chapter 4

There were six boys altogether, dressed in animal skins. Some of them carried clubs or swords. Others carried bows and arrows—not toys, but real wooden arrows with sharp flint arrowheads, the kind Lainey had only ever seen in books.

A boy with green eyes went to the table. "Who's been touching my mug?" he exclaimed, pointing to a gourd.

"Not me," said a boy who was dressed as

a raccoon. He turned to a curly-haired boy in bearskins. "Was it you?"

"Not me," said the curly-haired boy. He questioned a boy wearing rabbit ears in place of a hat. "Was it you?" And on they went, until each of the boys had denied touching the mug.

"Well, *somebody* moved it," said the green-eyed boy.

Beneath the bed, Lainey watched them in astonishment. All along, Lainey had thought that she and her friends were the only children on Never Land. And now to find out there was a whole pack of boys—the strangest boys she'd ever seen!

Just wait till Mia and Kate and Gabby hear about this! she thought.

"Maybe a rat moved it," suggested the curly-haired boy in bearskins.

"I'll get that rat!" said the green-eyed boy.

Lainey inched backward, trying to make herself as small as possible. It turned out to be a mistake. The movement caught the boys' attention.

They drew their weapons. "Come out, rat!" one of them shouted.

Lainey squeezed her eyes shut. She was done for! "I wish I'd never left Pixie Hollow!" she blurted out.

"That doesn't sound like a rat," one boy remarked, lowering his club.

"It doesn't look like a rat, either," said another, peeking under the bed.

The boys bent their heads together to discuss the situation.

"It said it came from Pixie Hollow!"

"It's awfully big for a fairy."

"It's not as pretty as a fairy, either."

"I can hear you, you know," Lainey said.

There was a moment of surprised silence. Then the boys continued their conversation.

"Do you think it might be a pirate?"

"Too small for a pirate."

"It's not as ugly as a pirate, either."

Lainey was getting tired of being talked about as if she weren't there. "I'm not a pirate," she called out. "I'm just a girl."

"What sort of girl?" one of the boys asked. "Mermaid or fairy?"

"Just a regular girl," said Lainey. She crawled out from beneath the bed.

The boys could not have looked more shocked if a talking turnip had popped up from the dirt floor. Their eyes grew round as nickels. Lainey noticed that most weren't much older than she was, and some looked younger. Suddenly, she felt much less frightened.

"My name is Lainey," she said. When

they didn't reply, she prompted, "What are your names?"

The boy wearing rabbit ears stepped forward. "I'm Nibs." He pointed to the tall, green-eyed boy in fox skins. "That's Slightly. The curly-haired one is Cubby. And these two you can't tell apart are the Twins."

A small boy wearing a skunk tail tugged Nibs's sleeve, then pointed to himself.

"Oh, yeah," said Nibs. "And this is Tootles. He doesn't talk."

Lainey laughed at the funny names. "What are your real names?" she asked.

Nibs lifted his chin. "My name's as real as my nose," he replied.

"Sure," Lainey said quickly, not wanting to hurt anyone's feelings. "I just meant, I've never heard names like those before."

"Peter gave them to us," Cubby said.

"Who's Peter?" asked Lainey.

The boys looked shocked. "Peter Pan, of course!" exclaimed one of the Twins. "He's—"

"Our captain!" the other Twin finished.

From the boys' proud faces, Lainey could tell they thought very highly of this Peter. She wondered what sort of captain he was—and what he would think of a girl showing up in his hideout.

As if he'd read her mind, Nibs said, "He's away now. But he'll be back in time for lunch. In fact, we were just on our way to get the rhinoceros."

Lainey raised her eyebrows. "You're having rhinoceros for lunch?"

"Of course not!" Cubby said with a snort. "You can't eat rhinoceroses. They taste awful!"

"We're having coconuts for lunch," Nibs said.

"We need the rhinoceros to ram the tree and knock the coconuts down. *Obviously,*" Slightly explained.

"A *real* rhinoceros?" Lainey had never seen a rhinoceros before. Suddenly, she wanted to see this one more than anything. But what if the boys wouldn't let her go with them?

"I can speak Rhinoceros, you know," she said quickly.

That wasn't strictly true, but it wasn't a total lie. Fawn was teaching her to speak (or rather, squeak) Mouse. And while not all animals spoke Mouse, of course,

Lainey had discovered that it was possible to squeak to a bear and make herself understood. She had never met a rhinoceros before. For all she knew, they spoke Mouse fluently.

Nibs looked impressed. "Well then," he said. "You had better come along."

Chapter 5

Prilla stood on a mossy bank above Havendish Stream. Down below, on the mudflats, the leapfrog race was in full hop. Animal fairies seated on frogs jumped over one another. Mud flew as they chased each other toward the finish line.

Fairies on the banks cheered for their friends. But Prilla was only half paying attention. Every so often, she fluttered up above the crowd to look for Lainey. She had been sure Lainey would show up to see her animal-talent friends race. But there was no sign of the girl.

With a last gigantic leap, one of the frogs sailed across the finish line. The rider was so covered in mud, at first no one could tell who it was.

"And the winner is . . . Fawn!" declared the referee.

As Fawn stepped forward to claim her prize, Prilla rose into the air. She would look for Lainey somewhere else.

As she flew, Prilla spotted Kate and Mia crouched beside the stream where the water ran fast. They were watching the leaf-boats dart over the rapids.

"Who's winning?" she asked, flying up to them.

"Rani was in the lead," Mia said. "But her leaf got stuck in a whirlpool. Now it's a tie between Silvermist and Marina."

"Go, Silvermist! Go, Marina!" Kate cried as the fairies flashed by in their maple-leaf canoes.

"I was wondering if you'd seen Lainey," Prilla said.

Before Kate or Mia could answer, Gabby ran up. "I won a prize!" she exclaimed.

"A prize for what?" Mia asked, surprised.

"Pea-shooting," Gabby said. "The garden fairies let me try."

"I thought the games were only for fairies," Kate said.

"They said I was an honorary fairy. I won third place!" Gabby held up a tiny ribbon no bigger than a daisy petal.

Mia and Kate laughed. "Gabby, you're ten times the size of a fairy," Kate said. "You only won third place?"

"I know I'm big," Gabby said. "But *they* have magic." Smiling proudly, she pinned the ribbon to her collar.

"Was Lainey at the pea-shooting contest?" Prilla asked.

Gabby shook her head. "Uh-uh."

"I thought she was at the leapfrog races," Mia said.

"I just came from there. I didn't see her," Prilla replied.

"Come to think of it, I haven't seen Lainey all day," Kate said. "She wasn't at lunch, either."

Prilla wrung her hands. "I'm afraid I might have something to do with that."

She explained what had happened earlier that day. "I didn't mean to hurt her feelings," she told the girls. "I was just scared and upset. I know it wasn't her fault. She didn't see me sitting there."

"I'm sure she'll understand if you tell her you're sorry," Mia said.

"That's what I want to do," Prilla replied. "But I can't find her."

"We'll help you," Kate said. "She must be somewhere around here."

The girls and Prilla looked for Lainey in all her usual spots. They checked the barn where Lainey liked to chat with the mice. They checked the tree where she picked her favorite pink-gold peaches and the mossy rock where she liked to lie on her back and watch flamingos fly past. But there was no sign of her.

As they were passing the willow tree, Mia suddenly had a hunch. She darted inside. The others followed.

"She's not here, either," Mia said as they came in.

"Do you think she went home?" Gabby asked.

Kate shook her head. "I can't believe she would leave without telling us."

"Well, she's not in Pixie Hollow," Mia said. "Where else could she be?"

"Look!" Gabby said suddenly, pointing to the trunk of the willow.

The others looked. "I don't see anything," said Kate.

"That's where her rope thingy usually

is," Gabby explained. "And it's not there
now."

"The harness. You're right!" Mia said.
"She must be out deer riding."

"By herself?" said Kate. "She never goes
without Fawn."

The girls and Prilla looked at each other. "Something is wrong," Mia said. "Lainey wasn't really acting like herself today."

"I noticed that, too," Kate said. "I wish now I'd asked her why."

"You don't think she's run away, do you?" Prilla asked.

"No," said Kate. "That's not like Lainey."

"She's not that reckless," Mia added, but she sounded uncertain.

"I'm sure she'll be right back," said Kate. "But let's check the forest, just to be sure."

Chapter 6

Lainey and the boys walked along single file. The forest seemed denser here than it had near Pixie Hollow. The air was hotter. The insects buzzed louder. Every now and then, an unseen animal screeched. The sounds made Lainey jump each time.

"How much farther is the rhinoceros?" she asked.

"Just a bit," one of the boys answered.

Lainey swiped a hand across her damp

brow. She was starting to believe that the boys had made the whole thing up and that there was no rhinoceros. Then, suddenly, they came into a clearing—and there he was.

Lainey had seen plenty of pictures of rhinos in books, but none had prepared her for the real thing. He was as big as a bull and looked twice as heavy. His cement-gray skin hung like armor. His tiny eyes sat low on his wrinkled head, which seemed weighed down by its enormous horn.

Lainey thought he was magnificent.

The rhino stood in the middle of a patch of tiny purple flowers. His eyes were half closed. He looked as if he might be dozing. On the other side of the clearing, Lainey spotted a tall coconut palm. Coconuts as big as basketballs hung beneath its leaves.

"What's the plan?" Lainey asked the boys.

From the way they looked at each other, Lainey realized they didn't have one.

"We could dig a hole in the ground and cover it with branches and leaves," Cubby suggested. "When the rhinoceros walks across it, he'll fall in."

"I thought of that," said Slightly.

"But that won't help us get the coco-nuts," one of the Twins pointed out. "And besides—"

"Wouldn't he notice us digging?" fin-ished the other.

"Exactly my thought," Slightly said, nodding.

"We could light the bushes on fire," one Twin said.

"And drive the rhino toward the tree!" added the other.

"I was just about to say that," said Slightly.

"But we might burn down the whole forest. Including ourselves," Nibs added.

"I knew it wouldn't work," Slightly agreed.

"What if you got the rhino to chase

you?" Lainey suggested. "Then you could lead him toward the tree so he would knock down the coconuts."

The boys thought this was a very clever plan. "Who volunteers?" asked Nibs.

They were all quiet a moment. Then Slightly said, "I volunteer Tootles."

Tootles looked taken aback. He pointed at Cubby.

Then Cubby volunteered Slightly. Slightly volunteered Nibs. And the Twins volunteered each other. Nobody wanted to be the one to rile up the rhino— not even Slightly, who claimed he'd thought of the idea first.

"If Peter were here, he would do it," said one Twin. Everyone agreed it was a shame Peter wasn't there.

Finally, Cubby said, "Why doesn't Lainey do it? After all, she can speak Rhinoceros."

All the boys looked at Lainey. She suddenly regretted her half-truth—which, now that she thought about it, was really more of a lie. But she didn't want her new friends to know she'd fibbed. And she didn't want them to think she was a coward. "Okay," she said. "I'll do it."

The boys all wanted to give her advice on what to say to make the rhino mad enough to chase her, so it was several more minutes before Lainey crept from their hiding spot in the bushes.

She stepped hesitantly into the clearing. The rhino was still sleeping. The only movement was the occasional twitch of his tail.

Maybe I don't need to make him mad, she thought. *Maybe I could just ask him nicely to knock some coconuts down from the tree.*

Lainey inched closer to the rhino. In a voice barely above a whisper, she squeaked in Mouse, "Excuse me."

Quickly, she stepped back, ready to run. But the rhino didn't move.

"Sounds more like a mouse than a rhino," Slightly remarked from the bushes.

"I don't think he heard you," Cubby called to Lainey. "Louder!"

"And maybe less squeaky," Nibs added.

Lainey's palms were sweating. This time, she lowered her voice to a husky squeak. "Hello there!" Her mouth was so dry she had to say it twice.

The rhino snoozed on.

Lainey relaxed. Either the rhino couldn't understand her, or he was sleeping too deeply to care. Showing off a little, she called, "Hey, you with the big beak!" She didn't know how to say "horn" in Mouse.

The rhino didn't even twitch an ear.

Lainey walked back to the boys' hiding spot. "It's no use," she told them. "I think he might be deaf."

The boys didn't reply. They were looking past Lainey with wide eyes. She spun around. The rhinoceros was awake—and he was looking right at her!

For a moment they stared at each other. Lainey took a step backward. The rhino took a step forward.

Lainey bolted—and the rhino charged! She could hear him thundering after her. For such a large animal, he was surprisingly fast.

The boys stood by, cheering like kids at a soccer game.

"Thataway, Lainey!"

"Faster, faster!"

"He's right behind you!"

"HELP!" Lainey yelled.

Then something amazing happened. Tootles leaped from his hiding spot. He began to swing his skunk tail and dance around.

The rhino stopped. It turned from Lainey and began to chase Tootles.

"Hey, you, you big lump! Over here!"
This time it was Cubby yelling. The
rhino started to chase him instead. Then
Slightly jumped in to save Cubby. The
Twins jumped in to save Slightly. Nibs
jumped in to save the Twins.

The rhino was getting confused. The
more confused he became, the madder he
seemed to get. Nibs wasn't far from the
coconut tree. But the rhino was quickly
closing the space between them.

"He's not going to make it!" Lainey
cried, covering her eyes.

The sound of the rhino's horn striking
wood rang out across the forest. Lainey
peeped through her fingers. Then she lowered her hands in amazement.

Nibs was sitting high up in the coconut

tree, while the rhino circled below. *How did he get there so fast?* Lainey wondered.

The rhino plowed into the trunk again. The tree swayed. The coconuts trembled. Nibs hung on for dear life.

With a third hit, a single coconut dropped to the ground.

The rhino seemed to feel he'd made his point. He turned and wandered into the forest without a backward glance.

When he was gone, the boys whooped and hollered and slapped each other on the back. Lainey couldn't even smile. It gave her goose bumps to think what a narrow scrape they'd had. She looked at the coconut on the ground. "All that for one lousy coconut?"

"Is that what's bothering you?" Cubby

asked. "Don't worry. Nibs will take care of it."

Sure enough, Nibs was picking coconuts and hurling them to the ground. Then he leaped from the tree. He swooped down as gracefully as a bird and landed next to Lainey.

"You can *fly*?" she asked.

"Oh sure," Nibs replied cheerily. "We all can."

"When we've got fairy dust, that is," Cubby added. "Sometimes it runs out. Then we have to wait for Peter to ask the fairies for more. But he left us with plenty."

Lainey couldn't believe what she was hearing. "Why did we risk our lives with the rhinoceros when any of you could have just flown up and picked the coconuts?"

The boys looked surprised. "What would be the fun in that?" asked Nibs.

Lainey stared at him. Then she started to laugh. "You're crazy," she said.

The boys laughed, too. Then they all sat down for lunch. It turned out to be quite a feast, for there is nothing like being chased by a rhino to work up your appetite. They ate three coconuts apiece.

They sat in the sun, patting their full bellies and talking about who had looked the funniest being chased.

For the first time all day, Lainey felt truly happy.

Chapter 7

"What should we do now?" asked Slightly.

Lainey and the boys were lying in the grass at the base of the coconut tree. They were all feeling sleepy from the sunshine and their big meal.

"How about a swim in the Mermaid Lagoon?" suggested Cubby.

"A swim? Oh no! We can't!" Lainey exclaimed.

"Why not?" asked Nibs.

Lainey thought quickly. "It's just that . . .

you can't swim for an hour after you eat."

Cubby frowned. "Says who?"

"Says my mom," said Lainey. "But every-body knows that. Didn't your mother ever tell you not to go swimming right after lunch?"

"Haven't got a mother," Cubby told her.

"Well, what about your dad?" asked Lainey.

"Haven't got one of those, either," said Slightly. "None of us do."

Lainey propped herself up on her elbows. "Then who looks after you? Your grandparents?"

"We look after each other," Nibs said.

"I don't mean here," Lainey said. "I mean when you go to your real homes."

The boys looked at her blankly. "But this is our home," Nibs said at last.

Suddenly, Lainey understood. The boys didn't travel back and forth through a magical portal. They lived in Never Land all the time.

"So you mean," she said slowly, "that you can do whatever you want? And there are no grown-ups to tell you what to do?"

"That's right," said Nibs. "Whatever we want. Whenever we want."

How wonderful! Lainey thought. No rules or bedtimes. No "dinner before you eat dessert" or "chores before you go out to play." It seemed like the perfect life. How could you ever have a bad day?

"Peter says that grown-ups are like flies on a cake. They just buzz around and spoil the fun," Cubby remarked.

Peter again! Lainey was getting more and more curious about him. "Where is Peter, anyway? Wasn't he supposed to be back in time for lunch?" she asked.

"He did say he'd be back for lunch," Nibs replied. "Though now that I think of it, he didn't say which day."

Even though they'd just eaten, the boys decided to swim anyway. They weren't inclined to listen to the advice of mothers, Lainey's or anyone else's. Lainey felt a knot in her stomach as they walked to the lagoon. She was sure they would laugh her right off the island when they saw what a terrible swimmer she was.

The lagoon was a white sand cove. Big rocks jutted out of the turquoise blue water. Lainey stood on the beach, toeing the sand, as the boys splashed into the waves. She tried to think of some reason why she couldn't go swimming.

I can say my stomach hurts, she thought. *Or my foot has a cramp. Or I'm allergic to water . . .*

Just then, she noticed something. Every boy was dog-paddling. Not one of them had his face in the water.

"What are you waiting for?" Cubby called.

"Come on, Lainey!" Slightly added. "The water's great!"

Lainey kicked off her shoes and waded in up to her ankles. The lagoon was warm as bathwater. With a joyful shout, she splashed in.

They took turns jumping off the rocks and seeing who could make the biggest splash. When they grew tired of that, they

played a long game of keep-away with a sea sponge, tossing it back and forth like a football.

As Lainey dove for a wide throw from Tootles, she suddenly found her head underwater.

She scrambled up to the surface, gasping. Then she paused for a moment, treading water. In the brief seconds she'd been under, she'd caught a glimpse of something amazing.

Did she dare look again?

Screwing up all her courage, Lainey took a big breath and stuck her face into the water. Far out in the lagoon, on the sea floor, was a brilliantly colored coral castle. It had sea-fan curtains and arched doorways. Large fish swam in and out of its open windows.

Lainey was entranced. She lifted her head out of the water, took a breath, then plunged back under to look again.

Nibs paddled over to Lainey to see what she was doing.

"What *is* that down there?" she asked him.

"Oh, you mean the castle? It's where the mermaids live," he replied.

Lainey realized they hadn't seen a single mermaid the whole time they'd been there.

"Where are they all?" she asked Nibs.

"They hide when we come swimming," he replied. "They're snobs that way. Peter's the only one they talk to."

Lainey was disappointed, until she found a starfish on one of the rocks. It was an especially pretty one—purple with green spots. Slightly was sure that a mermaid had worn it in her hair.

"Do you really think so?" Lainey asked, turning it over.

"Sure," said Slightly. "Mermaids always pick the best starfish for their hair. She probably left it behind when she was sunbathing."

Lainey put the starfish back on the rock so the mermaid would find it when she returned. She couldn't help thinking how much Mia would have liked to see the mermaids' castle.

After they'd finished swimming, everyone lay on the sun-warmed rocks to dry off. Nibs went up the beach into the forest and returned with a four-foot stick of sugarcane. He used his sword to cut off pieces, which he handed out.

"Can I see your sword?" Lainey asked as they chewed their sugarcane.

Nibs handed it over. The handle was made of brass and shaped like a dragon. "Where did you get it?" she said.

"From a pirate," Nibs replied.

Lainey raised her eyebrows. "A real pirate?"

"Of course!"

"He gave it to you?"

"Not exactly," said Nibs. "I won it in battle."

"Are there many pirates here?" Lainey asked.

"Sometimes," he replied. "They come and go. Right now they're off the island. Looting ships on the high seas, probably."

A shiver went down Lainey's spine. She wished Kate were there. She knew how much Kate would like seeing a real pirate's sword.

The truth was, Lainey missed her friends. But she was so much better off here. Here she wasn't Lainey-who-always-lost-her-glasses or Lainey-who-made-everyone-wait. And she certainly wasn't the "clumsiest Clumsy who ever lived." She was clever. She was brave. She had faced down a raging rhino and gone swimming in a mermaid lagoon and held a real pirate's sword. She was a girl who could do anything.

"I'm never going back," Lainey said to herself. "Not ever."

Chapter 8

Purple clouds streaked the sky as Prilla, Kate, Mia, and Gabby made their way through the forest outside Pixie Hollow. They had been following the deer trail for some time. But now that the sun had set, the path was harder to spot. No matter how she tried, Prilla couldn't glow much more than a firefly. She wished she'd thought to ask a light-talent fairy to come with them and brighten the way.

To keep their spirits up, Kate began to whistle. Mia joined in. Gabby couldn't whistle, so she sang. Prilla didn't know the girls' songs, so she clapped. Along they went through the darkening forest, walking in single file with Prilla darting among them. Despite the gloom, they made quite a merry little band.

They had just finished "The Hokey Pokey" and were starting on "Jingle Bells" when they heard a low growl.

The girls stopped walking. "What was *that*?" Mia asked.

Kate looked around. "Probably just a dog or something."

"The dogs in *our* neighborhood don't sound like that," said Gabby, huddling close to her sister.

"Prilla, are there dangerous animals on Never Land?" asked Kate.

"There are hawks and snakes, of course. And outside Pixie Hollow the crickets can be real brutes." Prilla shuddered. "No dogs that I know of, though."

"What about anything . . . *bigger*?" asked Kate.

"You mean like bears and wolves and crocodiles?" said Prilla.

"There are crocodiles?" Mia cried, putting an arm around Gabby.

"Just one," said Prilla. "Though he's pretty big."

"I wish we could go back to Pixie Hollow," said Gabby.

"But we can't," Kate replied, saying what they were all thinking. "Not until we find Lainey."

They went on. Kate began to whistle again, but no one joined her this time.

A sudden rustling in the leaves overhead made the girls jump. They stopped and peered up into the trees.

"At least we know that's not the crocodile," Kate said, trying to be cheerful. "*That* wouldn't be in a tree."

"It could be a panther," Prilla said. "I forgot about the panthers."

"Let's keep going," Mia said. "The sooner we find Lainey, the sooner we can get out of here."

They hurried along as quickly as they could, which wasn't very fast at all, since the forest was now quite dark. To lift their mood, Kate said, "Remember Lainey's dog treat stand? It was like a lemonade stand, except she was selling dog biscuits."

"I remember that!" Mia said. "No one in the neighborhood wanted to buy biscuits for their dogs. But Lainey didn't care at all. She just kept giving them away for free."

"She didn't make any money. But she made a lot of doggy friends," Kate said, smiling.

Mia smiled, too. "That's Lainey for you."

"Remember Lainey's first deer ride in Never Land?" Prilla asked.

"I do!" Mia giggled. "She was trying to say 'Giddy-up' in Deer—"

"But she ended up saying 'Fire!'" Kate broke in, laughing. "And the deer just took off! Lainey barely managed to hold on!"

"Remember when she talked to a bear?" Gabby said.

"I heard about that!" Prilla said. "It was the talk of the tearoom for ages. Lainey spoke to the bear in Mouse. What was it she said?"

"She said, 'I'm looking for my brothers and sisters,'" Gabby replied. "And the bear ran away. He thought we were great big mice!"

Everyone laughed.

Suddenly, Kate, who was leading, drew up short. They had come to a thorny thicket. The deer trail was gone. The girls couldn't see any way around or through the snarly plants.

"Now what?" said Mia.

There came a screech from the dark forest. The girls moved closer together. They took each other's hands. Prilla landed on Kate's shoulder.

"I'm sure it's nothing," Kate said uncertainly.

"I wish Lainey were here right now," whispered Gabby.

"So do I," said Mia.

"So do I," said Prilla.

"So do I," said Kate.

Chapter 9

Down beneath the forest floor, a party was taking place in the boys' underground hideout. As a cozy fire crackled in the hearth, Lainey and the boys made shadow puppets on the wall. They held handstand contests and jumped on the bed and tried to scare each other with their best ghost stories.

Lainey was having a great time. But she couldn't stop thinking of Kate, Mia, and Gabby and how they were missing all the fun.

She wondered what her friends were doing. They must have noticed she was gone by now. Were they worried? Had they returned home without her? Lainey was sorry she hadn't thought to leave a note.

Noticing the look on her face, Cubby stopped jumping. "What's the matter?" he asked. "Aren't you having fun?"

"Yes . . . it's just, I miss my friends," Lainey replied.

Hearing this, Slightly and Tootles stopped jumping, too. The Twins and Nibs came out of their handstands. "Were they good friends?" one of the Twins asked.

"Yeah," said Lainey. "And I left without saying good-bye."

"That sounds like a sad story," Cubby said warily.

"Cubby doesn't like sad stories," Slightly told Lainey. "They make him cry."

"Do not!" Cubby shouted, punching him on the arm.

"Do so!" Slightly said, pushing back.

"It's not all sad," Lainey said quickly. "We had lots of fun times, too."

Cubby nodded. "That sounds better."

"What sort of fun times did you have, Lainey?" one of the Twins asked.

They gathered around the hearth to hear the story. Only then did the boys realize that the fire had burned low and they were out of firewood.

They drew sticks to see who would go out to get more. Tootles lost. He gave

Lainey a mournful look, as if to say, "I always lose."

"I won't start the story until you're back," Lainey promised.

Tootles scuttled into the tree, and they heard him slowly climbing up to the forest.

He was gone only a few moments before he scrambled back into the room, gesturing madly.

"Somebody's coming!" Nibs translated. "Pirates, I think. Headed right this way!"

Tootles nodded. The other boys leaped to their feet. "If they've just come back to the island, they'll be looking for a fight," Slightly said.

"A fight with who?" Lainey asked in alarm.

"Whoever they find," Cubby said. "There's nothing like a few weeks at sea to make a pirate mean."

Lainey gulped. It was one thing to hear about a pirate battle. It was quite another to be mixed up in one. "Wouldn't it be better to stay in here, then?" she asked.

"And let them ambush us?" Cubby shook his head. "I say we sneak up on *them* first."

The other boys agreed. They began to gather their clubs and swords.

Lainey was in no hurry to go out into the dangerous night. On the other hand, she didn't want to stay there alone. She watched, uncertain what to do, as one by one the boys headed up to the forest.

Finally, Lainey and Tootles were the only ones left. He looked at her with raised eyebrows as if to say, "Aren't you coming?"

Lainey gazed longingly at the dying fire. How nice it would be to stay in this snug home. But then she thought of how Tootles had rushed out to save her from the rhino. It didn't seem right not to help him—and the other boys—now.

"All right." With a sigh, Lainey followed him, slowly climbing the notches in the hollow trunk that served as a ladder. But by the time she made it up to the forest, the boys, including Tootles, had vanished.

It was a moonless night. The forest was so dark that she couldn't tell where one tree ended and another began. "Tootles?" she whispered. "Nibs?"

Silence.

"Slightly?" she said, inching forward. "Cubby? Twins?"

"Shhhh," said a voice no louder than a mouse's sigh. A hand reached out and pulled her into the bushes.

The boys were crouched together there. They stared into the darkness. Lainey heard a tiny *snap,* like the sound of a twig breaking.

Pirates!

Nibs put a finger to his lips. Then, with a wave of his hand, he motioned the boys and Lainey for-ward. They began to sneak toward the pirates.

The sound of her own heart pounding filled Lainey's ears, so loud she was afraid the whole for-est could hear it. Her eyes had adjusted to the dark now. She could see three figures coming through the trees. They carried a single lantern between them. The lantern flame was so low it cast hardly any light at all.

There's something strange about that lantern, Lainey thought. It didn't swing like a lantern normally would. It moved up and down, this way and that, almost as if it had a mind of its own.

Just then, the light swung up high, and Lainey caught a glimpse of a face. She stood straight up and yelled, "STOP!"

But it was too late. With warlike whoops, the boys leaped out from their hiding place.

The pirates screamed.

The boys screamed, too, and jumped back in surprise. "Girls!" Slightly squealed.

The "pirates"—Kate, Mia, and Gabby— were standing there, clinging to each other in fright. What Lainey had mistaken for a lantern was Prilla, fluttering beside them.

When Kate heard the boys scream, she straightened and peered closer at the furry attackers. "They're not bears," she announced. "They're just boys!"

"I wouldn't say 'just,'" Cubby huffed, drawing himself up with as much dignity as he could.

Kate was about to reply, when she caught sight of Lainey. The girls rushed over to embrace her.

"What are you doing here?" Lainey asked, every bit as surprised as they were.

"Looking for you, of course!" Kate said. "What are *you* doing here?"

"And who are they?" Mia added,

pointing at the boys, who were watching with confused expressions.

Lainey made introductions. The boys were still suspicious. Slightly declared he thought the girls might actually be pirates in disguise. The girls were also wary, since they thought the boys had given them an unfair scare. But when Lainey explained that it had all just been a misunderstanding, everyone warmed up.

Of course, as soon as the girls heard about the hideout, they wanted to see it. The boys, who were proud of their home, were eager to show it off. Kate, Mia, and Gabby tried out all the mushroom stools and looked at the coat hooks and took turns making water run into the washbasin. They praised the boys' cleverness so much that even Nibs turned pink.

As they explored, Lainey told them about her day. Kate was thrilled to hold the pirate sword, just as Lainey knew she would be. Mia was delighted to hear about the mermaid castle. And Gabby liked the story of the rhinoceros so much she made Lainey tell it twice.

In the excitement, Lainey almost forgot about Prilla. When she finally thought to look for her, the fairy was flying out the door.

Chapter 10

Prilla flew into the dark forest. The night air was cool. It felt good after the warmth of the hideout.

She was glad to see the girls reunited, and relieved that everything had worked out. But it had been a long day, and she was eager to return to Pixie Hollow.

Still, she hadn't gotten a chance to apologize to Lainey. The girls and boys had been having such a good time, they hardly seemed to notice her. *Maybe it's better just to leave them to their fun,* she thought.

As Prilla hesitated, she heard footsteps behind her. She turned and saw Lainey. "Where are you going, Prilla?" Lainey asked.

Prilla flew over to her. "Back to Pixie Hollow. But I wanted to tell you that I didn't mean what I said about you being a clumsy Clumsy. I'd fly backward if I could."

"You really didn't mean it?" Lainey asked.

"Of course not!" Prilla exclaimed. "I was just upset. I was having a bad day. The worst day ever, in fact. I'm afraid I took it out on you. Please come back to Pixie Hollow."

"But what about the other fairies?" Lainey said.

"What other fairies?" Prilla asked.

"Everyone," said Lainey. "They must be laughing at me. They think I'm just a big Clumsy."

"No one was laughing at you," Prilla assured her. "I don't think anyone really noticed. They were all focused on the games."

Lainey thought about that. Maybe the fairies she'd heard hadn't been laughing at her after all.

"I'm sorry I almost stepped on you," Lainey said. "You were right to be angry. I should have watched where I was going. I was having a bad day, too. But it's turned into one of the best days ever. Isn't it funny how that works?"

Prilla agreed that it was.

"You know what I think?" Lainey said.

"Maybe bad days are just bad days. It doesn't mean everything is bad."

Prilla smiled. "I think you might be right about that."

Kate, Mia, and Gabby emerged from the hideout, followed by the boys. "Prilla, aren't you staying?" asked Kate.

Prilla shook her head. "It's time for me to go home. It's late, and there's something I still need to do."

"I'm ready to go back, too," Lainey said.

"You're really leav-ing?" Slightly asked.

"I thought you were going to stay here for good," said Cubby. He looked as if he might cry.

"Thanks, but I miss my home," Lainey told them, realizing it was true.

"But you'll come back for a real pirate battle, won't you?" Nibs asked.

Lainey smiled. "Maybe," she said. "But I might have to miss it. The thing is, I don't speak Pirate."

The boys and girls said good-bye and promised to meet again. Then the girls and Prilla started back toward Pixie Hollow.

"You know," Lainey said as they went along, "there's one thing I'm sorry about."

"What's that?" asked Prilla.

"The boys kept talking about someone named Peter Pan. But I never got to meet him," Lainey said.

"Oh," Prilla replied. "You never know. You still might get the chance. Anything is possible in Never Land."

*

Later that night, Prilla stood on a high branch of the Home Tree. Pixie Hollow was dark and quiet. The games were long since over. The ribbons had all been handed out. The sweet potato had been roasted and eaten. The girls had returned to their homes on the mainland. Now the fairies were tucked in their beds, worn out from the excitement of the day.

Prilla yawned. She was tired, too. But before she went to sleep, she had one thing left to do.

She sat down, settling her dress around her. She focused and took a deep breath. Then she blinked.

She was in the brown living room. The boy was sitting cross-legged on the floor. But this time he wasn't watching TV.

He seemed to be waiting for something.

When he saw Prilla, his face lit up. "I knew it!" he cried. "I knew you were real! I knew it was true!"

Prilla turned a cartwheel in the air, crying, "Clap if you believe in fairies!"

The boy clapped with all his might. Then he held out his hand, palm facing up. Prilla fluttered down and gently landed on it.

The boy brought her closer to his face. She heard him suck in his breath. His brown eyes were wide and full of wonder.

"Fairy," he whispered, "this is the best day ever."

Read this Sneak peek of
A Pinch of Magic,
the next Never Girls
adventure!

Tina and Tara Taylor sat on the porch swing, their long, straight blond hair pulled back into matching high ponytails. The girls were a year older than Mia and were identical twins. Even their grandmother had trouble telling them apart. To make matters worse, they always dressed exactly alike.

"Whatcha doing?" one of the twins asked.

"We just signed up to volunteer at the block party," Gabby piped in.

"Us too," said the other twin. "We're going to do the Bake Sale."

"So is Mia!" Gabby exclaimed.

"But I'm not—" Mia started to say.

"We're making Death by Chocolate Cake," said one twin, cutting her off.

Her sister elbowed her in the side. "No, Tina! We're making lemon meringue pie!"

"Wrong!" said Tina. "We decided on chocolate for sure." She eyed Mia. "What are *you* making?"

"Um . . . I don't know," Mia said.

The two girls came over to the front gate. Now that they were no longer sitting, Mia had mixed them up again. One of the sisters narrowed her eyes at Mia. "Well, I bet we'll sell more than you," she said. Mia smiled despite herself. The Taylor twins weren't just competitive with each other, they were competitive with everyone else, too.

"Wanna make a bet?" asked the other twin.

"Actually, I—" Mia started to say.

"Sure, we'll make a bet with you," Kate interrupted.

Mia shook her head at Kate. But Kate ignored her. She stepped forward and placed her hands on the fence. "Mia's going to beat you both, no problem," she added.

The twins whispered back and forth. Then they both nodded.

"Okay, Mia, if you lose you have to wear a T-shirt all week that says TARA AND TINA TAYLOR ARE THE BEST BAKERS ON SPRUCE STREET," a twin said.

"*Tina* and Tara," said the one who must have been Tina.

"And if ... I mean, *when* Mia wins," Kate retorted, "you both have to wear a T-shirt that says MIA VASQUEZ IS THE BEST BAKER ON SPRUCE STREET."

"Sure," Tina said with a smirk.

Mia and her friends started to walk away. "May the best baker win!" one of the twins called after them.

"Kate! Why did you do that?" Mia asked when they were out of earshot.

"Well, somebody had to take them down a peg," said Kate. "I can't stand how they're always whispering. They act like they're better than everyone else."

"But I can't win the bet. I don't know the first thing about baking!" said Mia. She had butterflies in her stomach. What had Kate gotten her into? And how in the world was she going to pull this off?